Dear Parents:

Congratulations! Your child is taking the first steps on an exciting journey. The destination? Independent reading!

STEP INTO READING® will help your child get there. The program offers five steps to reading success. Each step includes fun stories and colorful art or photographs. In addition to original fiction and books with favorite characters, there are Step into Reading Non-Fiction Readers, Phonics Readers and Boxed Sets, Sticker Readers, and Comic Readers—a complete literacy program with something to interest every child.

Learning to Read, Step by Step!

Ready to Read   Preschool–Kindergarten
• big type and easy words • rhyme and rhythm • picture clues
For children who know the alphabet and are eager to begin reading.

Reading with Help   Preschool–Grade 1
• basic vocabulary • short sentences • simple stories
For children who recognize familiar words and sound out new words with help.

Reading on Your Own   Grades 1–3
• engaging characters • easy-to-follow plots • popular topics
For children who are ready to read on their own.

Reading Paragraphs   Grades 2–3
• challenging vocabulary • short paragraphs • exciting stories
For newly independent readers who read simple sentences with confidence.

Ready for Chapters   Grades 2–4
• chapters • longer paragraphs • full-color art
For children who want to take the plunge into chapter books but still like colorful pictures.

STEP INTO READING® is designed to give every child a successful reading experience. The grade levels are only guides; children will progress through the steps at their own speed, developing confidence in their reading.

Remember, a lifetime love of reading starts with a single step!

Thomas the Tank Engine & Friends™

CREATED BY BRITT ALLCROFT

Based on The Railway Series by The Reverend W Awdry.
© 2015 Gullane (Thomas) LLC.
Thomas the Tank Engine & Friends and Thomas & Friends are trademarks of
Gullane (Thomas) Limited.
HIT and the HIT Entertainment logo are trademarks of HIT Entertainment Limited.
All rights reserved. Published in the United States by Random House Children's Books,
a division of Penguin Random House LLC, 1745 Broadway, New York, NY 10019, and in
Canada by Random House of Canada, a division of Penguin Random House Ltd., Toronto.

Step into Reading, Random House, and the Random House colophon are registered
trademarks of Penguin Random House LLC.

Visit us on the Web!
StepIntoReading.com
randomhousekids.com
www.thomasandfriends.com

Educators and librarians, for a variety of teaching tools, visit us at
RHTeachersLibrarians.com

ISBN 978-0-553-52168-9 (trade) — ISBN 978-0-553-52169-6 (lib. bdg.) —
ISBN 978-0-553-52170-2 (ebook)

Printed in the United States of America
10 9 8 7 6 5 4 3

HiT entertainment

THOMAS & FRIENDS

A Ghost on the Track

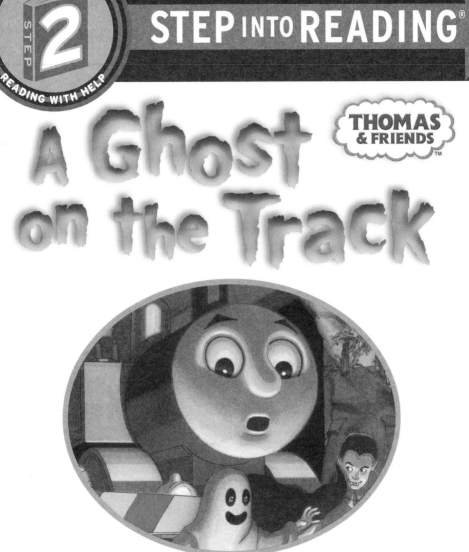

Based on The Railway Series
by The Reverend W Awdry

Illustrated by Richard Courtney

Random House 🏠 New York

4

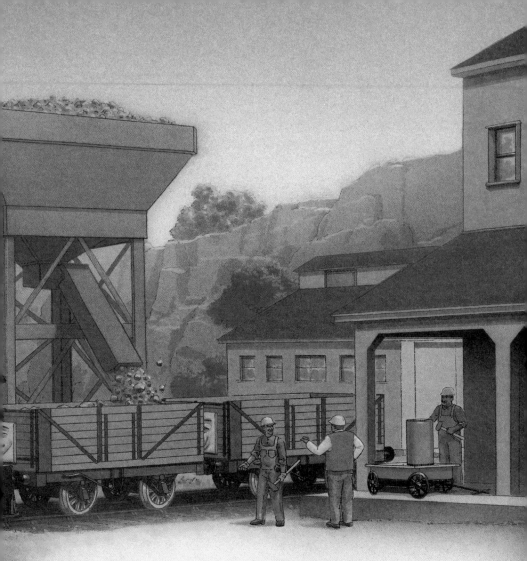

It is almost time
for Halloween
on the Island of Sodor!

Thomas looks at
the spooky decorations.

He thinks the scarecrow
is a little scary!

7

Thomas is on his way
to the Halloween party.

A black cat crosses
the track.
Thomas' Driver says
black cats are bad luck!

Gordon is slow.

Now Thomas is late.

Thomas thinks

he is having bad luck.

Bags of leaves
are on the track.
Thomas feels
even more unlucky.

At the station,
Thomas cannot see
the children
in their costumes.

Thomas thinks
black cats are
the worst luck ever!

Thomas' luck does not
get any better.

He has to stop again.

Bertie zips past.

Finally, Thomas gets
to the Halloween party.

He likes looking
at the costumes.

Thomas sees a ghost!
And another black cat!

Will Thomas' luck
get even worse?

Sir Topham Hatt has
a special Halloween
surprise for Thomas!

Thomas is happy
to meet little Thomas.
Little Thomas gives him
a shiny red apple.

Thomas finds Mavis
at the party.

He tells her about
little Thomas.
Thomas thinks about
the black cats he saw.

Thomas still thinks
the scarecrow is
a little scary.
But now he knows
that black cats are
good luck!